Boudicca
Strikes Back

Stories linking with the H~~~~~~~
National ~~~~~~~~~~~~~~~~~~~~~~ 2

D1589576

First published in 1999 by Franklin Watts
96 Leonard Street, London EC2A 4XD

Text © Natalie Grice 1999
Illustrations © Kate Sheppard 1999

The right of Natalie Grice to be identified as the Author
of this Work has been asserted by her in accordance
with the Copyright, Designs and Patents Act, 1988

Editor: Sarah Snashall
Designer: Jason Anscomb
Consultant: Dr Anne Millard, BA Hons, Dip Ed, PhD

A CIP catalogue record for this book
is available from the British Library.

ISBN   0 7496 3366 2 (hbk)
          0 7496 3546 0 (pbk)

Dewey Classification 942.01

Printed in Great Britain

Boudicca
Strikes Back

by
Natalie Grice

Illustrations by Kate Sheppard

W

FRANKLIN WATTS
NEW YORK • LONDON • SYDNEY

1
Romans

The Queen's eyes blazed.

"I said the red tunic," she stormed, "not the green!"

"Y–yes, your Highness." I quickly hunted through the clothes chest and pulled out a bright red tunic. It wasn't a good idea to keep Boudicca, Queen of the Iceni, waiting.

I had never seen a person like Boudicca. She was as tall as a tree with thick red hair that seemed to have no end. She had fair skin with big red lips and deep blue eyes – all three of them! I'm not joking. In the middle of her forehead she

had a dark blue eye tattooed. It was impossible not to stare at it when she spoke. She frightened me to death half the time, but I loved her as if she were a goddess. To me, it was the highest honour to serve as her handmaid.

Boudicca finished dressing and placed her golden torc around her neck. Then she stood in front of the polished bronze mirror. She looked wonderful in her long crimson tunic.

"Oh, you look beautiful!" I blurted out, before I could stop myself. I wasn't supposed to speak, and I waited to be told off. But Queen Boudicca turned to me with a smile. "Thank you, Callie," she said, as she left to go to the courtroom. That was just like her. Scream at you one minute, praise you the next. Life was never dull with Boudicca.

About an hour later, I had just finished tidying the bedroom when I heard a terrible noise in the hall. I peeked my head around the curtain. There were Roman soldiers pouring into the hall! One of Boudicca's guards tried to stop them and was knocked down. I could hear loud voices in the courtroom.

I tiptoed up to the curtain at the back of the courtroom and crept inside. Boudicca was standing with both hands at her hips, one resting on the handle of her long ceremonial sword. A group of Roman soldiers stood in front of her.

"What do you think you're doing?" she shouted. "How dare you steal things from my kingdom! My people say –"

"Your kingdom? Your people?" The captain of the group laughed. "Everything belongs to Emperor Nero now. When your husband died, it became Roman property."

Boudicca snapped back, "My husband left half of his money to the emperor, nothing else!"

The captain, at least a head shorter than Queen Boudicca, waved his hand in the air. "Be quiet, woman. I've heard enough of your chatter."

Oh dear. Now he'd done it. Boudicca seemed to swell to twice her size. "Woman?" she repeated. "You can't speak to me like that!" She lifted her arm and smacked him hard across the face.

The courtroom exploded. There was a roar of "Seize her!" and the next thing I

knew the Romans had dragged Boudicca outside to the busy courtyard. They threw her sword to the ground. Then one soldier pulled a whip from his belt. I quickly hid my face in my hands and turned away.

After what seemed like hours, I heard

the captain say, "That'll teach her a lesson she won't forget. Let's go." I looked up as the Romans ran to their wagons and drove away, loaded down with goods belonging to the Iceni tribe.

Boudicca was lying on the floor. Her pretty tunic was torn at the back where the whip had touched it. Slowly, she reached out and clutched her sword. Using it as a support, she forced herself

upright. Everybody was still. Leaning on the sword, she faced the shocked people around her.

"Those Romans have taught me a lesson," she snarled. "They've taught me that Romans are liars who can't be trusted! I kept quiet before. But now … enough is enough!

"We have put up with these bullies for too long. I am going to drive them from this land or die in the attempt!" She looked around. "Are you with me?"

Together, everyone shouted, "We are!"

We were going to war!

2
To war

Boudicca sent messengers all over the land to leaders of other tribes. She asked them to come to a meeting – a council of war, she called it. It was held on the hill above our town. I had never seen so many people together before. There were lots of different tribes – the Trinovantes, the Catuvellauni, the Durotriges, the Dobuni, the Brigantes, and more. They had one thing in common though. Everyone spoke of their hatred for the Romans.

Boudicca stood up at the front of the crowd. She looked very serious.

"My friends," she boomed, her powerful voice clear to everybody, "the time for battle has come.

'You know that the Romans have built a new capital town called Camulodunum. That's where the soldiers who attacked me

came from. Well, now all the troops there have gone to fight another tribe, who live a long way from here. This is our chance to destroy Camulodunum.

"At the edge of the town is the Temple of Claudius. The Romans are very proud of their wonderful temple," she spat fiercely. "I want every stone knocked to the ground!" We all cheered.

Boudicca continued, "We are going to kill every Roman we meet! And anyone who works with the Romans. They're just as bad!  Death to all traitors!" Hunting horns were blown. The noise was deafening!

Boudicca put her hands up and silence fell. "We must attack soon. But first we need to frighten the Romans. Frightened people are easier to beat. I am going to send them a prophet who will tell them that trouble is coming. Somebody who seems innocent. Somebody they will trust."

She was looking in my direction. I looked behind me to see who this person was. Nothing there but a tree. I turned back. She was still looking at me. And so was everybody else … !

"Callie," the Queen boomed, "you will go to Camulodunum and tell the Romans that trouble is coming. You are going to be the Iceni's first spy."

3
Callie the spy

I was standing on a hill looking down at
Camulodunum!

"Andate, Goddess of Victory, help
me!" I prayed.

It had all happened so fast! One
minute I was an unknown maid making

the beds, the next I was a spy going to
fool the Romans. Boudicca's parting
words filled my ears: "Callie, I know I can
trust you like a daughter." Why me? I'd
never been outside our village before. I
was terrified!

I looked at the Roman town. It was so
big! There were hundreds of buildings in it.
The streets ran in straight lines across and
down. There was a huge stone building on

the far side. That must be the Temple of Claudius that Boudicca had talked about. I stared in amazement.

It was five times the height of a man! There were lots of thick, round pillars at the front. They were like stone trees. I had never seen anything like it. Clearly the Romans could do more than just fight.

I gathered all my courage and set off into the town. There were lots of people around. Some of them looked like me. Others were very different. They had

darker skin and hair, and lots of them had
brown or black eyes. I had never noticed
what size the Romans were before. Roman
soldiers wore helmets which made them
seem tall. These ordinary Romans were
tiny! I wasn't fully grown yet, but some of
the men were even shorter than me. And
the clothes were so funny! The men were
wearing full-length cloaks which only
fastened over one shoulder.

The street I was following opened out
into a large, noisy square. It was about ten

times bigger than the yard outside
Boudicca's hall! There were a lot of
buildings on all sides, with people hurrying
in and out. None of the buildings looked as
huge as the temple though.

The square was very busy. There were
lots of different stalls with men and women

hard at work buying and selling food,
animals and cloth. I stopped to look at one
of the food stalls. Some of it was the same

as I would eat at home, but there were some very strange-looking fruits – or were they vegetables? I wanted to taste them but I had no money and nothing to barter with.

Suddenly I remembered I was here to do a job, not to go shopping! With my whole body shaking, I chose a space near to the stalls, took a deep breath, and opened my mouth to speak. No words came out. I swallowed and tried again.

Nothing! My mouth was refusing to work. I cleared my throat and had another go. "Sqwalk," I said.

This was terrible. Here I was trying to do my first job for the Iceni, for Queen Boudicca, and I had failed before I started.

Just then, a long line of men crossed the square. They were all carrying a heavy load of stones on their backs. The men looked tired and ill. They weren't small Romans. They were Trinovantes, the people who had lived here before the Romans came. On each side of the line were two soldiers. They had swords at their sides and whips in their hands. One of the men carrying stones stumbled and dropped his basket of stones. Straight away, a soldier hit him with the whip! The

man didn't make any noise. He just picked up his basket and carried on walking. I was shocked. I remembered the soldiers who had whipped Boudicca. Would the Iceni become Roman slaves too? Not if I could help it!

I threw back my head. "Beware! Beware! Beware!" I yelled. "The town is cursed. The food is poisoned. Everybody will suffer terrible pain. The sky is falling

down." I didn't know what I was saying.
But it had an effect on the people nearby.
They stopped what they were doing to
listen to me. I carried on shouting
nonsense. More and more people gathered
around. To make myself look more like a
prophet, I closed my eyes and lifted my
hands in the air, the way the Druid priests
in our village did.

"Birds bigger than houses will drop
giant eggs and crush the town. Rocks will
grow teeth and bite your legs off. The river

will turn into blue snakes! Run away!" I cried. I rocked from side to side and wailed a few times. A few voices from the crowd wailed back. I moaned and screeched loudly. They screeched louder! I could hear the panic spreading all around the market place. I was scaring them all right. This was great fun!

Fun, that is, until somebody grabbed my wrists and lifted me off the ground. I opened my eyes. A fierce pair of brown eyes stared down at me from under a metal helmet. It was a soldier!

"You're coming with me!" he barked.

4
Arrested

Two soldiers dragged me through the market place. I kicked and struggled my hardest but it was no use. "Help!" I shouted. Nobody paid any attention. The soldiers marched me along street after street. I was frantic! Where were they

taking me? And what were they going to
do with me?

We arrived at a
row of huts inside a
courtyard. They
opened the door of
one and threw me
inside. I fell to the
floor.

One of the
soldiers
grinned evilly
at me. "You
can shout all you

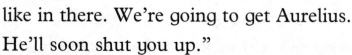

like in there. We're going to get Aurelius.
He'll soon shut you up."

He slammed the door shut and I heard
a bolt being drawn. I was trapped in the
dark. The only gleam of light in the hut
came from the crack between the door and

the frame. But that
was enough to show
me the rats crouching
at the back of it!
Earwigs ran up my
legs. Something landed on
my head. I brushed it off. Eek! It
was a big, black cockroach.

This man, Aurelius, must be somebody
important. And what
did the soldier
mean when he
said Aurelius
would shut me
up? Shut me up
permanently? I
felt sick with fear.
I couldn't tell if I
had been locked in
this hut for minutes or hours.

At last the door rattled and opened.

"Get her out," a voice said.

The soldier from the market place ducked in and yanked me out. I blinked hard in the sunlight.

Standing in front of me was a man wearing the funny one-shouldered cloak. I've said that Romans were small. He must have been the smallest of them all!

His arms and legs were thinner than mine! A few strands of oily hair flapped around his lined face. I nearly burst out laughing. Surely this couldn't be Aurelius?

The soldier spoke.

"Aurelius, this is the girl we found causing trouble in the forum. She was speaking of bad things happening. Shall we get rid of her?" he asked, putting his hand on his short, sharp sword.

Suddenly, I didn't feel like laughing.

Aurelius stared up at me. I knew he only had to click his fingers and I'd be killed. He didn't look funny anymore. I was more afraid of him than of the soldiers. I quickly said a silent prayer to

Andate – and all the other gods I could remember. Just as I was about to give up hope and get ready to join the spirit world, he spoke.

"No," he said. I sagged with relief. "I  want to know what she was doing." Uh-oh! Aurelius looked hard at me. "Well? I'm waiting."

"I – um." What could I say? "I say things. And then the things I say come true."

Now he looked interested. "A voice from the gods! In my town! Tell me, what did they say to you?"

"They said ... they said the tree of knowledge will flower in five days and let loose the seeds of doom." I tried to look mysterious.

Aurelius nodded his head slowly. "The seeds of doom? That's – very interesting." It was? He continued. "And you say you can see the future?"

"Yes."

He had a crafty look on his face. "You could be very useful. As of now, you're working for us. I'm going to make a Roman out of you."

"B-b-but," I stammered, "I don't want to be a Roman!"

Aurelius laughed. "You don't want to be a Roman? Don't be ridiculous, girl! Everybody wants to be a Roman. We're the most powerful people in the world!"

"Why? Because you make everyone else into slaves?" I snapped without thinking.

Aurelius's face went white with anger. "You'll be a Roman," he growled, "or you'll be dead!"

5

The house of Aurelius

Aurelius took me to his house. It was
made of stone and you had to climb a few
steps to go in the front door. I had a
surprise when I stepped inside. Even
though it was quite a cool day, the floor
was warm! I stared at the ground.

Aurelius noticed.

"You've never been inside a Roman house before, I suppose." I shook my head. "It's much better than the simple things your people build. Do you know why the floor is hot? It's because there's a space underneath the floor which is heated with hot air. We call it a hypocaust."

It was very pleasant to walk on, I had to admit. But then I remembered the slaves in the square. Probably men like those had built this house. With soldiers holding whips to their backs!

"Julia!" Aurelius called. A serving

woman came rushing into the room.

"Julia," he said, "this girl will be living here from now on. She's very important to me. She's got a gift Rome can use. Get her a decent tunic. She can't work for a Roman while she's wearing those clothes. If she gives you any trouble, let me know." He turned to me. "And don't forget – you've frightened the whole town with your prophecies. If they're  true, you better start asking the gods for a way for us to save ourselves. Otherwise you're no use to me – understand?"

Oh no. Things were getting worse!
Julia took me into a small room which had
some furs on the ground. "You can sleep
there," she said, and she left the room. She
came back carrying
a tunic over her arm.
"Put this on."

I hesitated. She
folded her arms.

"Remember what
the master said," she
warned. I took my
dress off. Julia lifted
the tunic over my
head and fastened it tightly around my
waist. The material felt lighter, smoother
and better woven than anything I had
worn before. There were buttons at the
shoulders and it had no sleeves. It felt very
strange wearing Roman clothes.

"You stay here," she said. She closed the door behind her and I heard the clunk of wood hitting wood. I pushed the door. It was barred. I was stuck here. I sat down on the furs and thought and thought and thought. But I couldn't think of a plan! I realised I was tired. I lay down. Just five minutes rest. Just … z z z z z z.

Boudicca's army was advancing across the plain. I watched as thousands and thousands of men, women and children, horses, wagons and cattle moved towards me. And at the head of the column was

Boudicca, her hair streaming behind her, a spear in her hand. She was saying something. "Death to all traitors. Death to anyone who wears Roman clothes. Death to Callie!"

I woke up in a panic! It was just a dream! But it would happen for real very soon. I had to get out! But how?

6

Boudicca attacks

The next few days were terrible. I was made
to work cleaning the house during the day.
All the doors were locked at night. There
seemed no way out.

Then one morning, as I was emptying
rubbish out of a window, I happened to look

up. The hill above Camulodunum was crowded with people. It was Boudicca's army, just as I'd pictured it in my dream.

Other people had seen it too. Romans were running up and down the street in panic. I could hear chariots rumbling, and the beat of horses' hooves.

Smoke was rising from the edge of the town. I'd be burnt along with the Romans if I stayed here.

It was time for a message from the gods! I banged the table and started to shout, "Ow! Ooh! Yeah! The gods are speaking." Aurelius came running in. I launched into my act. With my arms flying and my eyes rolling, I yelled, "Fire and destruction will eat this town. The sacrifice must be made. Let a young maiden find a two-headed, six-legged purple duckdog, and offer it to us. The rain will fall! The fires will die! The

attackers will be washed away. Do it, or all Camulodunum is lost!"

With that I fell to the floor moaning. I kicked my legs a few time then lay still.

It had quite an effect on Aurelius. He had stood with his mouth wide open during my performance. Now he came racing to my side and picked me up off the floor.

"The gods have sent us a way out!" he cried. "We can still destroy the barbarians.

I knew you'd be useful."

I blinked my eyes a few times. "What happened? What did I say?"

Aurelius looked hard at me. "Girl, this is very important. Do you know what a duckdog is?"

I looked scornful. "Everybody knows what they are! They've got two heads, six legs and they're bright purple. They live in the forest outside Camulodunum. Why?"

Aurelius clapped his hands together. "Excellent!" He gave me that hard stare again. "Girl, I order you to go and get a

duckdog and bring it back here. As fast as you can!"

I pretended to look frightened. "But Sir, what about the barbarians?"

"NOW!" he roared.

"Yes, Sir! Right away!"

I ran to my room, grabbed my old clothes and stumbled out into the street. There was a big smile on my face. He'd fallen for it! I was free!

7
Victory

It was madness on the street. People were running in all directions, some holding weapons, some pulling animals behind them. One woman had a cooking pot in each hand!

I hesitated for a moment on the steps

of Aurelius's house. What was the best thing to do? Should I try and get out of Camulodunum? Should I try and find Boudicca and her troops?

Just then, four men carrying swords came round the corner. They were Iceni tribesmen! I was saved!

"That's it!" called one of the warriors. "That's where the chief of Camulodunum lives."

"Look, there's a Roman girl on the steps," said another.

"It must be his daughter, trying to

escape. Let's pay him back for all the children we've lost. Get her!"

"No, no!" I squealed. "You're making a mistake! I'm not Roman!" I cried. "I'm Callie, the queen's –"

They put their swords in the air. "CHARGE!"

There's only one thing to do when a warrior shouts 'Charge'. Run!

I bolted down the street. The swordsmen were hot on my heels. I turned left, right, left. So did they! Thank the gods they were carrying heavy swords and shields. It slowed them down just enough for me to keep ahead of them. But I couldn't keep running for ever.

I dodged into a side alley. Had I lost them?

I had to get this tunic off while I had the chance. I pulled at the knotted belt.

It was tied so tight I couldn't undo it. I tried to tear it but I just wasn't strong enough. A knife or a sword would cut it. I could hear a lot of noise coming from the next street. Maybe I could find one there.

I ran round the corner and fell flat on my face. I had tripped over somebody's legs. I didn't wait to find out if they were alive legs or not!

The road I was on was very wide, and filled with people. Fights were happening everywhere. And at the end was the Temple of Claudius! Boudicca's number one target. Warriors were hammering at the walls and door. They were trying to knock it down. As I watched, panting hard – CRACK! – they broke the door open. People poured into the building.

"There she is!"

Time to go! I pelted into the building
along with the crowd. The swordsmen
followed. I had to fight my way through
the crush of people. They were gaining
on me! I bumped into something
hard. I looked up. It was a statue.
Without thinking, I climbed up it
as fast as I could. Maybe
the swordsmen
couldn't climb?

Bad guess!
The leader of
the group
reached the
bottom and
looked up with
a grin on his face.

"We've got you now, little Roman," he
said. He put his sword down and placed
his hands on the statue's legs.

Then, like a miracle, a woman
appeared in the doorway. She was dressed
in a multi-coloured tunic, a twisted gold
crown on her head. Boudicca!

"QUEEN BOUDICCA, HELP ME!"
I screamed.

The swordsman paused.

"CALLIE!" Boudicca's powerful voice rang out through the building. "THE ICENI'S LITTLE HEROINE!"

She came striding through the crowd to the statue I was sitting on.

"I knew you wouldn't fail me, Callie! And look at you. Disguised as a Roman, you clever girl! Sitting on the head of the Emperor Claudius in triumph! What a day for the Iceni!"

I had been saved by the statue of a Roman emperor! I laughed aloud.

Boudicca lifted me down. "Stand back everybody," she commanded. She lifted her sword above her head in a sign of victory. Then she swung it at the statue. There was a huge crash! The statue's stone head fell to the floor. The crowd roared with joy. We had won!

Boudicca

Boudicca lived in Britain at the time of the Roman conquest in AD44. She became queen of her Celtic tribe, the Iceni, after her husband Pratusagus died. The Iceni lived in the part of Britain we now call East Anglia. Roman writers of the time say that Boudicca was a big, strong woman with long red hair and was very brave.

In AD60 she led a massive attack against the Romans. Many other Celtic tribes fought alongside Boudicca against the Romans. The Romans were unpopular rulers. They stole land and made people slaves, and this made the British tribes angry.

The fight against the Romans

Boudicca and her army attacked Camulodunum (known today as Colchester). They killed all the twenty thousand people who lived there, and burnt it to the ground. They then did the same thing at Londinium (London), and then Verulamium (St Albans). However, these places were undefended towns. In order to get rid of the Romans for good, Boudicca had to defeat the Roman army.

The battle took place somewhere in the middle of England. The Celts had between three and five times as many fighters as the Romans, but they couldn't beat them in a battle.

The Roman soldiers were trained to fight as a team and to obey orders. The Celts were fearless fighters but they weren't organised properly. Boudicca's troops were all killed by the Roman army. Boudicca herself took poison, rather than be captured by the Romans.

Roman ways

The Romans were more advanced than the Celtic tribes of Britain (although it didn't stop them from being very cruel sometimes). Some of the roads and buildings they made still survive today, two thousand years after they arrived in Britain.

The Romans invented the first form of central heating, called a hypocaust. Roman buildings had a space under the floor. Fires were lit in this space and the hot air from the fires warmed the floor, making it easier to live in a cold country like Britain!

Roman beliefs

The Romans believed in lots of different gods.
They built temples in praise of all kinds of gods.
Usually, once the ruling Emperor died, he was
made into a god. This is what had happened
at Camulodunum. The temple there was
built to honour Emperor Claudius, who
had been the ruler of the Roman
Empire at the time of the invasion of
Britain in AD44.

Sparks: Historical Adventures